MW01053030

Claire Goes Foraging

Margaret Aycock

Copyright © 2015 Margaret Aycock
All rights reserved.
ISBN:1502792125
ISBN-13: 9781502792129

ClaireGoesForaging.blogspot.com

DEDICATION

To mothers, grandmothers and great grandmothers who passed along their knowledge of the plants of the woods and fields to us, who had a great respect for the earth and all that it could provide for us; nourishment, healing and shelter.

To a mother and father who allowed us children to play in, and explore the mountains, woods, fields, and streams, and in so doing, gave us a great appreciation for the natural world, and a desire to preserve it.

For my husband who accompanies me any time I get a hankering for a walk in the woods, and who is a relatively willing participant in my foraged food cooking experiments.

Special thanks to my great niece, Claire, and my friend, Charica for modeling for the characters in this book.

FOREWORD

I remember finding sassafras in the woods as a young girl. I brought a twig home to show to one of my farming neighbors who identified it, and helped me to make sassafras tea from the roots. I remember the good feeling I had drinking that warm tea and knowing that I found, and made it myself.

Years later another neighbor shared with me her knowledge of wild food which had been passed down to her by Cherokee and African American grandmothers.

I have been serving my family foraged food for as long as I can remember, sometimes gathered from fields and woods near our home, but often gathered right out of our lawn and vegetable garden where I allow poke sallet, dandelion, wild onion, lambsquarters to grow wherever they wish to plant themselves.

When I harvest from my own yard, whether garden vegetables, or wild plants, I know the food I find will be fresh, not genetically modified, and will be pesticide, and herbicide free.

I find that now when I take a walk into the woods or fields around my home, I am much more observant, and present to the bounty that is available to me.

It wasn't until I started doing research for this book that I found that the readily available, wild plants that I knew to be delicious, were also extremely high in nutritional value, often containing much higher concentrations of vitamins and minerals than store bought vegetables.

I also wanted to mention that for the purposes of this book I am including only a sampling of the most commonly found edible wild plants. All included plants have passed the test of being very recognizable, tasty, and nutritious. None have any poisonous lookalikes, or require special preparations such as multiple boilings, in order to eat. All of the greens included here can be eaten raw but the palatability of some improves with cooking. If you don't like them raw, throw them in the soup pot.

Most of the included greens can be interchanged in recipes with other familiar ones such as spinach, kale, and lettuce. You may wish to start by interchanging only small amounts.

I encourage you to experiment, and like Claire, expand your knowledge using the internet, books or by my favorite way, learning from a grandma, a neighbor, a friend, who knows what is safe and delicious to eat.

Claire Goes Foraging

Claire woke in the morning to the sound of her father mowing the yard outside her bedroom window. Remembering that today was the day that her father had promised a trip to the ice cream shop, she quickly dressed and ran downstairs for breakfast.

On the kitchen table was her dad's list of Saturday chores. She knew there would be no ice cream until all the work was done.

After making a peanut butter and jelly sandwich for breakfast she grabbed her camera and ran outside where her father was now working in the garden.

She had her own list of chores which involved taking pictures of butterflies and other insects for her scrapbook. She thought that the garden would be a good place to start.

"So have you come out to help your dear old dad in the garden?" her dad asked with a grin.

"No," she laughed, snapping a quick picture of a butterfly that had just landed on a yellow dandelion flower. I've come to take pictures for my scrapbook, but I can help you too."

 As the butterfly flew away her father, digging deep with his garden trowel, pulled up the dandelion, roots and all, and tossed it onto a pile of other plants that were destined for the compost pile.

 "Why are you throwing that flower away?" Claire asked.

 "I am weeding the garden," he replied, and that plant, including its pretty flower, is a weed."

Claire looked confused.

He continued, "Any plant growing in the vegetable garden that we don't use for food is a weed, even if it is pretty. I pull them up because they steal nutrients from the soil which are meant for our vegetables. I want our tomatoes, broccoli, spinach and beans to get all the nutrients they need so they can grow big and tall. Then, when you eat the vegetables that we grow, their nutrients will help you get big and tall." He paused, "Now, since you offered to help, and you seem to know what dandelions look like, would you like to be in charge of pulling up all the dandelions?"

"They will be easy to find," Claire said as she put down her camera and picked up the blue garden fork.

Before long Claire spied their neighbor, Celeste, just beyond the garden wall, and asked, "Daddy, may I go over to see Celeste?"

"Sure," he said, as he waved hello to Celeste.

Claire snatched up her camera and ran across the yard to join Celeste.

It appeared that Celeste was also weeding her garden and yard, but unlike her father, Celeste was gathering the leaves without the roots, and putting them in a big red bowl.

Claire easily recognized the leaves as dandelion.

"Daddy says you have to pull up the roots too or they will grow back," said Claire as she knelt beside her neighbor.

"That is true," answered Celeste. "but I want them to keep coming back, because the tender leaves and buds are very nutritious. I am picking some for a salad that I am making for supper."

Claire was puzzled. As she looked into the red bowl she recognized other plants that looked like the ones her father had just thrown onto the compost pile.

"I thought all those plants were weeds." Claire said as she pointed to the greens gathered in the bowl.

"Well, some people now days seem to think so, but your ancestors, and mine ate them all the time. They survived on food they found by foraging in the woods, prairies, lakes, and streams. The earth provided for them very well. If it had not, you and I wouldn't be here at all. Eating these plants helped our ancestors grow strong and healthy, and helped to heal them when sick or injured."

"The secret of which plants were edible, and which were good for healing was passed down from grandmother, to mother, to daughter in my family, for many generations."

"A secret!" thought Claire. "Can I know the secret too?" she asked.

Celeste stopped a moment to think . "I don't have a daughter to pass the secrets to, but I will gladly teach you what I know, if you would like to learn," she said, giving Claire a little hug.

"Oh, I do, I do!" said Claire excitedly. "When can we start?"

"Right now, if you would like to," said Celeste. "You could start by helping me gather some wild plants for tonight's supper. Do you think your dad would like a home cooked meal tonight if you and I worked together to prepare it?"

"I think he would," Claire hesitated, "but maybe we shouldn't tell him that he is eating weeds," she smiled.

As Claire ran across the yards to ask her father if she could spend the day with Celeste, Celeste called across the wall to him, "If you would let me borrow Claire for the day, we can promise a delicious meal for all of us, for supper tonight."

"I am sure Claire would love that, and dinner sounds great! What would you like for me to bring?" he asked.

"Why don't you surprise us with something from your garden, and we will surprise you with something from my garden," she suggested.

"It's a deal," he said.

"I see you have your camera, Claire. That will be a great tool to help you remember the different plants that I want to show you."

Claire thought out loud, "Maybe I could put them in my scrapbook too, with their names, and how to cook them."

Celeste smiled at her willing student. "That is a great idea, Claire, and I can help you with that when we go inside. Are you ready to take your first picture?"

"Let's start with something you already know, the dandelion. Why don't you take a picture, and later, I will give you the recipe for the wilted dandelion green salad that we will have for supper tonight. When we go inside I can also help you find some information on the computer about the nutritional value of the plant, and you can add that to your scrapbook too."

After gathering enough dandelion greens and buds for their salad, Claire asked, "What other plants are we going to use for supper?"

Dandelion

Dandelion is real easy to recognize. It has yellow flowers that turn into little white puff balls after a few days. I like to blow on the puff balls because when I do, a lot of little seed parachutes float through the air.

You can eat the leaves and the flower buds.

You should pick the leaves when they are small because the bigger ones can be more bitter. Gather them year round. Some say they are better in the spring.

You can cook them like greens or make a delicious wilted dandelion green salad. Some people take the stem part of the leaves off before they cook them. You can put them in smoothies too.

They have lots of vitamins and minerals in them; Vitamins A,C,E,K,B6,B1,B2. Dandelions are also a good source for folate, magnesium, phosphorous, copper, calcium, iron, protein, and antioxidants.

They are also good for lowering cholesterol and regulating blood sugar, and insulin.

They are a diuretic and very good for digestion too.

Wilted Dandelion Green Salad

6 slices of bacon
1 onion
2 garlic cloves crushed
2 tsp brown sugar or more to taste
2 TBs vinegar
a bunch of young greens with the stem removed
salt and pepper to taste
Cook the bacon and remove.
Add onion and garlic to the bacon grease and
cook on low heat till onion is translucent. Add vinegar
and greens. Top with chopped bacon.
Salad should be served warm.

" We need to gather several different greens for a casserole, and some for a second salad. We will also gather some wood sorrel, and sumac berries for 'lemonade,' she said as she started across the far side of the lawn.

They headed towards a group of short tree like plants with big clusters of bright red berries on them.

"Let's start by gathering some of these pretty red sumac berries. This plant is very easy to identify, especially in the late summer and fall," she said, while pulling a cluster down to give Claire a closer look.

She then picked one of the berries and handed it to Claire. "Touch your tongue to this and tell me what you taste."

Surprised, Claire said, "It tastes just like lemons!"

Celeste suggested, "Let's put some of them in our bowl and then I will show you another plant that is tangy like a lemon."

Claire paused to take another picture for her scrap book before following Celeste to the edge of the lawn.

Sumac

Sumac bushes are very tall. The ones in Celeste's yard are over her head and she says they will get taller. They have big clusters of red berries on them in the late summer and fall. The clusters are bigger than your hand and are kind of sticky and very, very lemony. You can make a cold drink like lemonade out if it in the summer and a hot drink in the winter. You can dry and grind the berries to use as a lemon like spice all year round. The berries have a lot of vitamin C in them.

Sumac Lemonade

Several bunches of sumac berries
honey or sugar
a cup or so of wood sorell leaves, stems, flowers
water
You can also add mint leaves

You can make this like sun tea by letting the berries and wood sorrel steep in a glass jar outside in the sun for a few hours or by pour boiling water over them and let the mixture sit inside until cooled. Strain the berries and sorrel out by using a colander and cheese cloth or just use a colander. What you will have left is a pretty red lemonade. Add more water and honey to taste.

You can also drink this as a hot tea in the winter. You could add rose hips to the tea too.

"We still need wood sorrel for our lemonade. See if you can find a plant that reminds you of a three leaf clover, or a shamrock," said Celeste as she paused near a patch of plants that had bright green leaves and little yellow flowers.

Claire remembered looking for four leafed clovers with her friends, who thought that finding one would bring good luck.

As Claire knelt to snap a picture Celeste told her that the stems, leaves, flowers and seeds are all edible.

Hearing that, Claire popped a leaf into her mouth. She puckered her lips and made a face. "It tastes sour like a lemon too!" she exclaimed.

"Yes it does, and that is why I often use it in recipes that call for lemons, like lemonade. Let's gather a few of the leaves for our lemonade and then we will find some of the ingredients for our casserole."

"Now we are going to look for one of my very favorite greens. I like it because it grows all summer and into the fall and just keeps getting bigger and bigger. I just gave you a hint to help you find it. It is the tallest plant in my yard except for the trees. See if you can spot it."

Claire pointed to the far side of the yard where she spied a plant that was taller than her dad. It had light, dusty bluish green leaves all over its many branchlike stems.

"You are exactly right," said Celeste. "You have found my lambs quarters. We will need a lot of them for the dish we are going to make. When we look this up on the computer you will see how very nutritious this plant with the funny name is."

Just then Celeste stopped as she saw something at the edge of the garden.

"Oh my, what a find! This is purslane, the most nutritious of all my wild treasures. It is even more nutritious than any of the greens that grow in your dad's garden."

Lambsquarters

Lambsquarters were some of the easiest weeds to find because they were taller than me! The leaves are kind of a dusty blue green color. The leaves and the seeds are good to eat but Celeste says she leaves the seeds for the birds to eat in the winter. The leaves are full of vitamins A and C, calcium, phosphorus, potasium, protein, niacin, fiber, and omega 3 and omega 6 fatty acids.

Spanakopita with mixed greens

2 lbs of spinach and mixed greens (purslane,
lambs quarters, violet leaves)
2 cups feta cheese
2 cups cottage cheese
5 eggs
1 cup chopped onion
2 Tbs flour
2 tsp dried basil (or 1/4 cup fresh)
1 tsp dried oregano (or 1/8 cup fresh)
3 Tbs butter
filo dough and more butter (melted)
salt/pepper
Turn oven to 375 degrees.
Cook onions in butter till soft and turn off the flame.
Throw the greens in the pan and put a lid on it.
After a few minutes add wilted greens to the bowl with
the other ingredients and stir it up.
To assemble start by putting some melted butter on
the bottom of a casserole dish. Add a layer of filo.
Brush the top with butter and add more filo, brushing
between each layer till you have 6 layers. Pour in your
other ingredients. Top with 8 more buttered filo layers.
Fold layers in at the edges and pop it in the oven for
45 minutes.

Celeste held up a pretty little plant with leaves that looked to Claire like little beaver tails.

"We will have to make a special little salad with purslane for tonight's dinner," said Celeste. "There are many other plants that grow wild in our yards that we can pick another day but I think we have gathered enough for today. Let's take these into the house and get started," she said as she picked up the red bowl and headed towards the house.

As they passed by the stone wall she paused. "There is one more thing I want to show you."

"I bet you never thought you could eat flowers, did you?" Stopping just under a trellis of climbing roses she asked with a twinkle in her eye, "Can you guess which ones are my favorites?"

"Roses!" shouted Claire.

Purslane

Purslane is really good for you. You can cook it or eat it in a salad. You can eat the leaves, stems, yellow flowers, and seeds. The leaves are a little crunchy and tart if you don't cook them. Here are some of the good things that are in purslane: VITAMINS ! Lots of vitamin A, C, and omega 3 fatty acids. (It has the highest amount of omega 3 than any other leafy green.) MINERALS! Calcium, potassium, magnesium.

Purslane Tomato Salad

2 cups of sliced cherry tomatoes
3/4 cup of feta cheese cut into 1 inch pieces
1 cup purslane leaves
1/2 cup fresh basil leaves
1/2 cup black olives
1/2 cup green olives
1/2 cup of chopped onion
4 garlic cloves crushed
1/4 cup olive oil
1/4 cup balsemic vinegar
salt and pepper to taste
Stir ingredients together and marinate in the refrigerator for at least 1/2 hour.

"Yes, you guessed right. I like to put rose petals in my salad, and sometimes, violets, because they look so pretty. Later on in the season I will gather the fruit of the rose plant, rose hips, for my winter tea, but for now, why don't we just pick some roses to enjoy in a vase."

Claire took the red bowl while Celeste cut some roses, and they went inside to work on Claire's scrapbook and their evening meal.

That night Claire's dad arrived with a big vegetable casserole to add to the wonderful dishes created by Celeste and Claire. They all agreed that it had been fun to make a meal from food that they had grown or gathered themselves.

Claire's dad said the salads and casserole were delicious and asked what ingredients were in them. Claire told her father all about how she and Celeste foraged for wild plants that they used in their recipes, and how they made 'lemonade' without using lemons, just like the Native Americans did.

He laughed in surprised when Claire told him that he had eaten 'weeds' like dandelion, purslane, and lambs quarters.

She showed him her scrap book pages with all she had learned about wild plants and nutrition. As he read what she wrote, he was even more surprised to learn that the foraged plants that he had eaten for dinner were also very nutritious.

In all the excitement of the day, Claire had almost forgotten the thing that made her jump out of bed that morning until her father turned to them and asked with a big grin, "Did anyone save room for an ice cream cone?"

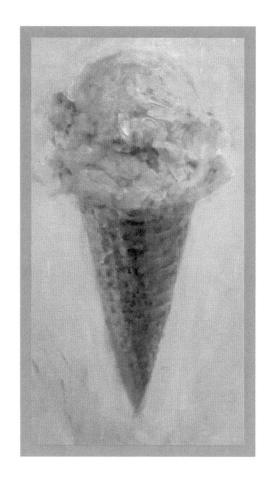

The End

MAKE YOUR OWN SCRAPBOOK ON THE FOLLOWING PAGES WITH PICTURES AND
RECIPES THAT YOU LOVE

MY FORAGING SCRAPBOOK

MY FORAGING SCRAPBOOK

40918189R00026

Made in the USA
Lexington, KY
03 June 2019